DATE DUE		

791.43 Perlman, Marc.   10385
PER
         Movie classics.

**MESA VERDE MIDDLE SCHOOL
POWAY UNIFIED SCHOOL DISTRICT**

390104 01624   13729A   11

M·O·V·I·E
CLASSICS

M·O·V·I·E CLASSICS

by Marc Perlman

Lerner Publications Company
Minneapolis

Page 1: Al Pacino as Michael in *The Godfather*; **page 2:** Charles Foster Kane campaigns for governor in *Citizen Kane*.

Copyright © 1993 by Lerner Publications Company

All rights reserved. International copyright secured. No part of this book may be reproduced or transmitted in any form or by any means, electronic or mechanical, including photocopying and recording, or by any information storage or retrieval system, without permission in writing from Lerner Publications Company, except for the inclusion of brief quotations in an acknowledged review.

LIBRARY OF CONGRESS CATALOGING-IN-PUBLICATION DATA

Perlman, Marc, 1961-
  Movie Classics / by Marc Perlman.
    p. cm.
  Includes index.
  Summary: Describes and analyzes seven classic movies, from *Metropolis* to *Annie Hall,* and places them in the context of cinema history.
    ISBN 0-8225-1641-1
  1. Motion pictures—Evaluation—Juvenile literature. 2. Motion picture plays—History and criticism—Juvenile literature.
[1. Motion pictures—History.] I. Title.
PN1995.9.E9P4   1993
791.43'75—dc20
                                        92-30909
                                            CIP
                                             AC

Manufactured in the United States of America

1 2 3 4 5 6 98 97 96 95 94 93

Contents

Introduction 7

Metropolis 11

Gone with the Wind . . 19

Citizen Kane 29

The Manchurian Candidate 39

Psycho 49

The Godfather Epic . . 59

Annie Hall 69

For Further Reading . . . 78

Index 78

The classic horror movie *Psycho* (1960) still terrifies audiences.

Introduction

Have you ever talked with your friends about a movie and heard someone say, "That one's a classic"? Usually another person replies, "Well, it's a good movie, but it's not a classic." When it comes to movies, the label "classic"—which means a work of enduring excellence—often starts an argument. Of the thousands and thousands of movies that have been made during the last 100 years, only a handful deserve the title classic.

What makes a movie a classic? Movies are made up of many different elements, including acting, screenplay, special effects, camera work, and direction. If you add the elements of a movie together, and the result is a work that both critics and audiences think is unique, important, and entertaining, you might have the makings of a classic.

Of course, a movie that seems great and important to one person may seem boring or meaningless to someone else. One viewer might think the camera angles used in a

Is *Close Encounters of the Third Kind* **a science fiction classic? You be the judge.**

movie are artistic, while another viewer might consider them silly. Even a film's message may seem positive to one person but negative to another.

A good example of a movie that many people viewed differently is *Close Encounters of the Third Kind*. The movie, about a visit to Earth by aliens, featured fantastic special effects and fine acting. Some critics liked the movie's message that humans can benefit from learning about other worlds in the universe. Audiences loved the movie.

Many people consider *Close Encounters* to be a classic science fiction movie. Others disagree. They think *Close Encounters* involves too much fiction and not enough science. The movie "uses the trappings of science," one critic wrote, "to deliver the strongly anti-science message of pie-in-the-sky."

Critics and audiences often disagree with each other about movies. Most critics praise European directors such as Jean-Luc Godard and Wim Wenders. But American audiences are often bored and confused by "overintellectual" European movies. Ironically, American audiences and movie critics think comedian Jerry Lewis's movies are stupid, but the French consider Lewis a comic genius.

If a movie is popular with audiences *and* critics, it has a good chance of making movie hall-of-fame status. But a movie must pass one final test—after the reviews have come in and the money has been counted—before it can be called a classic: It must stand the test of time.

A movie might be called a classic when first released, but then be forgotten—or even criticized—10, 20, or 50 years later. The 1915 silent movie *Birth of a Nation*, for instance, was ahead of its time in the use of film techniques. But many people now call the movie racist because of its presentation of the Ku Klux Klan. As people's attitudes about the world change, so do their attitudes about movies.

Some movies, like *Birth of a Nation*, lose stature over the years. Other movies don't get the credit they deserve until years after they are made. Many critics loved *Citizen Kane* when it came out in 1941. But audiences did not flock to theaters to see it, and the movie was virtually ignored at the Academy Awards ceremony that year. *Citizen Kane* was soon forgotten.

Yet, 50 years later, *Citizen Kane* is considered one of the greatest movies of all time. It is as sophisticated as the European classics, but it also addresses popular American themes of power, love, and money. Director Orson Welles's filmmaking techniques have inspired other great directors like Martin Scorsese and Woody Allen. *Citizen Kane* is a true classic because it has survived the test of time.

Only one movie in history, *Gone with the Wind*, was considered a classic right away. It remains a classic to this day. But even a movie that stands the test of time and is loved by reviewers and audiences might still invite controversy. Some people feel that *Gone with the Wind* doesn't deserve to be called a classic because of its outdated and offensive messages about slavery.

Why does *Gone with the Wind* still pack in viewers while other famous movies do not? What makes a movie a classic?

Let's take a look at seven famous movies and try to find out what makes each a classic. But remember, the best way to decide if a movie deserves to be called a classic is to see it for yourself.

Note: The following abbreviations are used in this book:
b/w black and white
dir director
pro producer
sc screenplay by
st starring

(1927)
METROPOLIS

b/w
dir Fritz Lang
sc Fritz Lang and Thea von Harbou
st Gustav Frohlich (Freder Fredersen), Brigitte Helm (Maria), Heinrich George (Grot), Alfred Abel (John Fredersen), Rudolf Klein-Rogge (Rotwang), Theodor Loos (Joseph)

Metropolis is one of the greatest science fiction movies of all time. It is also one of the greatest movies to come out of the silent-movie era (1900–1930). Director Fritz Lang's innovative use of special effects, lighting, and set design changed the way movies were made forever.

Metropolis's message about the triumph of the human spirit over technology is just as relevant in the 1990s as it was in the 1920s. The story takes place in the futuristic city of Metropolis. Citizens who have been born into wealth and power control the technology in Metropolis. They live high above the city in luxurious skyscrapers.

The workers live below the surface of Metropolis. They are treated like animals. The rulers of Metropolis force the workers to live underground so the wealthy people will not have to see how the workers suffer.

When *Metropolis* was made, workers all over the world were fighting for better working conditions and higher pay. The movie showed how bad the future could be if relations between workers and industry leaders did not improve. *Metropolis* tells audiences that love must bring the hands of the workers and the brains of the rulers together.

The city of the future: Metropolis

Metropolis explored the connection between technology and human relations in a way that movies had never done before. And Fritz Lang explored the connection between filmmaking and technology like no other director before him. His special effects—images of giant industrial machinery and flying machines zipping around huge skyscrapers—were technically and visually innovative. The most exciting special effect in *Metropolis* is when a frightening metallic robot turns into a human character before the audience's eyes. Lang's images of the futuristic city were copied in sci-fi movies for many years, as was his use of mirrors, models, and other visual tricks.

The mood of *Metropolis* is dark and depressing. But the love story between the son of the master of Metropolis and the leader of the workers is uplifting. *Metropolis*'s political and social messages are still important to moviegoers.

"Who told you to destroy the machines, you fools—and thus yourselves?"

Inside the underground factory that powers the futuristic city of Metropolis, workers, all dressed in the same drab uniforms, operate huge machines under terrible conditions. The rulers of Metropolis live high above the city.

Freder Fredersen, son of the master of Metropolis, is in a garden. A young woman enters, surrounded by dirty orphans. Freder asks who the woman is.

She is Maria, the daughter of a worker. Freder, smitten by Maria's beauty, follows her out of the garden. He finds himself in the huge factory below the city. A worker who is in charge of keeping the machinery cool is dying. The machines overheat and send shock waves through the factory. Many workers fall to their deaths from the platforms where they work.

Freder is upset by this tragedy and races to the offices above the city to see his father, John. But John Fredersen does not care about the workers' safety. Freder, disgusted with his father, goes to work in the factory himself.

Meanwhile, Grot, the foreman of the central factory tells John that the workers are plotting to take over the factory. John goes to see Rotwang, an inventor who has created a robot that will replace the workers. The robot will look exactly like a human being.

Freder and the workers meet in the catacombs, the underground tunnels below the city. Freder sees Maria standing with her arms outstretched. She tells the crowd that a mediator must bring peace between the workers and the rulers of Metropolis. "Be patient, he will surely come," she says.

John and Rotwang hear Maria's speech too. John tells Rotwang to make his robot in the image of Maria. The robot will impersonate Maria and lead the workers to revolt. John will use the rebellion as an excuse to kill the workers.

Rotwang abducts Maria and brings her to his house. Freder walks by the house and hears Maria's screams. He searches for her but cannot find her.

Rotwang has hooked Maria up to a huge machine that will turn the robot into a likeness of Maria. With lights flashing and liquids boiling, rings of energy surround the robot. It slowly takes on Maria's image.

"Go down to the workers and undo Maria's teachings," John tells the robot. "Stir them up to criminal acts." The robot Maria nods obediently.

Freder sees the robot and starts to hallucinate. His head spins with images of his father, Maria, and death. He sees Maria in a belly dancer's outfit and a transparent shroud, dancing wildly for the leaders of Metropolis.

Rotwang and his robot. In *Metropolis* advanced technology threatens to kill the human spirit.

Meanwhile, Rotwang is telling the real Maria about John Fredersen's plan. Maria has always preached patience and nonviolence to the workers. But now John and Rotwang are using her image to incite violence.

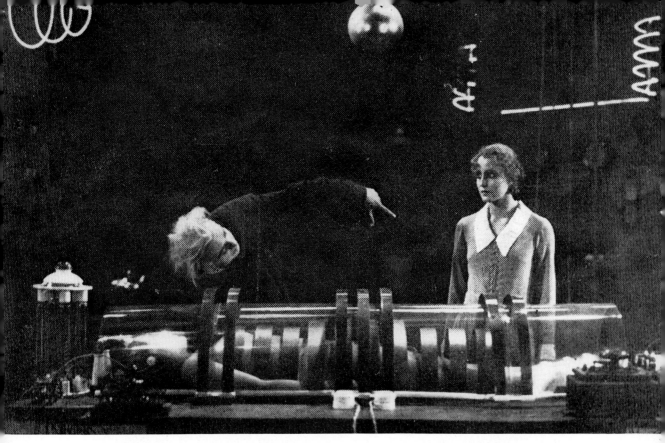

Top: In his laboratory, Rotwang makes his robot look just like Maria.
Bottom: Freder and Maria must save the children from the flood.

The robot Maria tells the workers to rebel against the leaders of Metropolis. "I have preached patience," she tells the attentive workers. "But your mediator has not come—and will never come."

Meanwhile, Freder is in his plush room above the city. A friend, Josef, tells Freder what is happening underground. They rush down to the catacombs, where the robot Maria is working the crowd into a frenzy. "You are not Maria!" Freder yells to the robot.

Some of the workers attack Freder and Josef. Others carry off the robot Maria and head for the factory. The foreman tries to stop them, but the workers destroy the machines, causing the underground city to flood.

The real Maria escapes from Rotwang's house as the flooding begins. She rushes to save the workers' children and is joined by Freder and Josef. Together they lead the children to safety.

John learns about the flooding. Realizing that he has caused the destruction, he grabs his head and screams in anguish. Meanwhile, the workers realize that they have destroyed their own homes, and they burn the robot Maria.

Rotwang tries to kill the real Maria, but Freder stops him. The workers, along with John, watch the struggle. When Rotwang falls to his death, John goes down on his knees in thanks.

Maria pleads with Freder to unite the workers and the masters of Metropolis. "There can be no understanding between the hands and the brain unless the heart acts as a mediator," she tells Freder.

With one hand, Freder takes his father's hand and with the other he takes Grot's hand. He brings the two men together and in doing so creates a new future for all of Metropolis.

VISIONS OF THE FUTURE

Metropolis was the first movie to recognize the influence of technology on everyday life. *Metropolis* and many science fiction movies that followed warned that technology could be dangerous.

Many science fiction moviemakers were inspired by Fritz Lang's vision. *Blade Runner* (1982) is the story of a police officer (Harrison Ford) who tries to track down rebellious androids in Los Angeles in the year 2019. Like *Metropolis*, *Blade Runner* presents a bleak vision of the future—one in which society is divided into the rich few and the poor multitudes. The major corporations that control the world in *Blade Runner* remind us of John Fredersen in *Metropolis*.

One of the most frightening movies about the future is based on George Orwell's book *1984*. Written in 1948, the book tells of a futuristic society in which emotions have been outlawed and the government, called "Big Brother," uses advanced technology to invade and control the private lives of the people.

The movie *1984* was released in 1984. While some people breathed a sigh of relief in 1984 that the society of the late 20th century was not as bad as Orwell's vision, many people believed that some of Orwell's predictions had come true. Much of the technology we see in futuristic movies eventually becomes reality. Classic movies about the future tell us that the future is not as far away as it seems.

(1939)
GONE WITH THE WIND

color
dir Victor Fleming
pro David O. Selznick
sc Sidney Howard
st Vivien Leigh (Scarlett O'Hara), Clark Gable (Rhett Butler), Leslie Howard (Ashley Wilkes), Olivia de Havilland (Melanie Hamilton)

The release of *Gone with the Wind* in 1939 was one of the highlights of motion picture history. Both *Gone with the Wind* and the book by Margaret Mitchell that the movie was based on became instant classics.

The movie takes place in Atlanta, Georgia, during the Civil War between the northern and southern states. Before filming even started, *Gone with the Wind* received more publicity than any movie ever had before—thanks to producer David O. Selznick's nationwide search for an actress to play the role of the courageous southern belle Scarlett O'Hara.

Selznick put together the best cast and crew that money could buy. Clark Gable as the swashbuckling Rhett Butler and Vivien Leigh as Scarlett became as legendary as their characters. The relationship between Scarlett and Rhett is a classic story in movie history.

Gone with the Wind showed viewers both the elegance of the Old South and the horror of the Civil War.

Thanks to Selznick's attention to detail and the talents of everyone behind the scenes, *Gone with the Wind* looks like it was really filmed in Civil War Georgia. Every scene, set, and detail—from the burning of Atlanta to Scarlett's plantation home, from the costumes to the accents—were made as realistic as possible.

But the character of Scarlett touched audiences more than anything else. Moviegoers fell in love with Scarlett and her fight to survive the horrors of war, the loss of her family, and the destruction of the southern way of life.

Scarlett O'Hara is unlike any other 1930s movie heroine. She seems selfish and uncaring. But these same qualities enable her to survive the destruction of everything she loves. She is also independent, smart, and courageous. To many, Scarlett is film's earliest feminist.

Gone with the Wind used great filmmaking techniques to tell a meaningful and dramatic story. The movie means as much to contemporary audiences as it did to viewers in 1939. It reminds us how war destroys the lives of millions of people. Ironically, when *Gone with the Wind* came out, World War II was just beginning.

"The cause of living in the past is dying right in front of us."

In 1861 the people of Atlanta, Georgia, are preparing for war with the Union army of the North. Young Scarlett O'Hara lives at a beautiful southern plantation named Tara. Scarlett is in love with a man named Ashley Wilkes, but Ashley is going to marry Melanie Hamilton.

At a party at Wilkes's plantation, Twelve Oaks, Scarlett notices a handsome stranger, Rhett Butler. Rhett has a bad reputation. He angers the men at the party by saying the South will lose the war.

Scarlett tells Ashley she loves him, and Rhett overhears the conversation. He says that Scarlett should love him, not Ashley. "You aren't fit to wipe his boots," Scarlett shoots back.

The men learn that war has begun, and they all hurry to enlist for the Confederate army of the South. Melanie's brother, Charles, asks Scarlett to marry him. She reluctantly agrees, even though she's in love with Ashley, who marries Melanie. Later, Charles dies of pneumonia.

Scarlett goes to Atlanta to visit Melanie. She again meets Rhett and again they do not get along. The South is losing the war, and many lives have been lost. Rhett thinks the war is a waste of life.

At Christmas Ashley comes home from the war. Before he leaves again, he tells Scarlett: "We shall need all our prayers now. The end is coming."

"The end?" Scarlett asks.

"The end of the war," Ashley says sadly, "and the end of our world, Scarlett." Ashley makes Scarlett promise to take care of Melanie while he is gone. Scarlett tells him that she married Charles just to make him jealous. But Ashley just says goodbye.

The Union army is shelling Atlanta. Scarlett and the other civilians try desperately to tend to the wounded soldiers. But Atlanta has run out of food and supplies. Scarlett cannot take the suffering anymore and decides to go back to Tara. But Melanie is about to give birth, and, remembering her promise to Ashley, Scarlett stays to help her. Scarlett delivers Melanie's baby.

After 35 days, the shelling stops. The streets of Atlanta are filled with injured and dead Confederate soldiers, as far as the eye can see.

Scarlett makes Rhett take her, Melanie, and the baby to Tara. Somehow they avoid the Union soldiers and reach the plantation. But Rhett decides to join the Confederates and he leaves them.

Tara is almost destroyed. Scarlett's mother is dead; her father is crazy. The Yankees (Northerners) have taken everything, including all the food. Scarlett, raising her fist to the sky, declares, "If I have to lie, steal, cheat, or kill—as God is my witness—I'll never be hungry again!"

Scarlett starts to put Tara back in order. The South has been defeated, and Ashley comes home from the war. Scarlett realizes she can never have Ashley. She marries Frank Kennedy for his money—so she can pay the taxes on Tara.

Scarlett is now cold and ruthless. When Frank is killed by some Northerners, Scarlett marries Rhett. Rhett is rich; Scarlett will use his money to rebuild Tara.

Scarlett and Rhett live in Rhett's mansion in Atlanta. They have a baby girl. But Scarlett still has feelings for Ashley. She treats Rhett poorly.

The Yankees attack Atlanta and leave the city in flames.

Rhett wants a divorce, but Scarlett is pregnant again. She says she does not want the baby. "Cheer up," Rhett says. "Maybe you'll have an accident." Scarlett swings a fist at Rhett and misses. She falls down the stairs.

Scarlett lies in bed, delirious, calling for Rhett. Rhett feels guilty for joking about Scarlett having an accident. He tells Melanie that he was jealous because Scarlett has

The stormy love affair between Rhett Butler and Scarlett O'Hara made superstars of Clark Gable and Vivien Leigh.

never cared for him. Melanie tells Rhett that he is wrong and should be patient.

Scarlett recovers. Rhett suggests they go on a second honeymoon. While they talk, their daughter is killed in a riding accident.

Melanie is dying. Scarlett walks out of Melanie's bedroom and, seeing Ashley, breaks down in his arms. Rhett is hurt and leaves.

Scarlett tells Rhett that she truly loves him and apologizes for the way she treated him. "You think that by saying I'm sorry, all the past can be corrected," Rhett tells her.

Rhett walks out on Scarlett. She chases him down the stairs. "If you go, where shall I go? What shall I do?" she cries.

"Frankly my dear, I don't give a damn," Rhett answers.

Scarlett looks up and, thinking of the one remaining thing in her life that means something to her, she finds strength. "Tara! Home. I'll go home. And I'll think of some way to get him back. After all, tomorrow is another day!"

MAKING *GONE WITH THE WIND*

The story of *Gone with the Wind* began long before the cameras started rolling. When a young woman from Atlanta named Margaret Mitchell broke her ankle, she decided to pass the time while she recovered by writing a romance novel.

Mitchell had no intention of having the book published, but her husband convinced her to send it to a publishing company. The publishing house accepted Mitchell's manuscript and then sent it to MGM Studios, where it landed on the desk of one of David Selznick's assistants, Kay Brown. At first Selznick was not interested in the story, but Brown finally convinced him to buy the movie rights.

Gone with the Wind was published in 1936 and won the Pulitzer Prize for fiction in 1937. Public anticipation for the movie was high—but it was about to become higher. David Selznick decided to turn the search for Scarlett into the greatest publicity stunt in movie history.

Selznick sent his assistants all over the country, the South especially, to find the perfect Scarlett. Moviegoers were asked to write in and vote for their favorite actresses. The press followed the voting as closely as it followed presidential elections.

Selznick really had no intention of "discovering" an unknown actress to play Scarlett. He was actually having every young, up-and-coming actress in Hollywood take screen tests for the role. Everyone from Bette Davis to Katharine Hepburn to Lucille Ball tried out, but Selznick was not satisfied with any of them.

Finally, Selznick announced that he had found Scarlett. He had decided to film the burning of Atlanta scene before an actress had been chosen, the newspapers explained. While the fire lit up the night sky, Selznick noticed a young actress, Vivien Leigh, who was a guest on the set. Selznick saw the flames reflected in her eyes and realized that Leigh was the Scarlett O'Hara whom Mitchell had described in her book.

The public loved the story. It seemed like a fairy tale come to life. In fact, it really was a fairy tale. Selznick had already decided on Leigh after seeing her in British movies like *Dark Journey* (1937). He invited her to the *Gone with the Wind* set and pretended that fate had brought Vivien Leigh and Scarlett O'Hara together. Despite the deception, Leigh's performance as Scarlett left no doubt that Selznick had made the right choice.

David Selznick created amazing scenes, like the burning

Southern belles attend a party at Twelve Oaks.

of Atlanta, on the lots of MGM Studios in Los Angeles. The buildings were really just plywood fronts left over from other movies. But the talents of people like production designer William Menzies and art director Lyle Wheeler convinced audiences that the action was really taking place in Civil War Atlanta.

For the burning scene, fires were lit in hundreds of gas pipes throughout the fake buildings. The blaze was so large that many Los Angeles residents thought their city was really burning! William Menzies choreographed hundreds of extras, running through the movie-lot streets, to give the impression that the whole city of Atlanta was in turmoil.

To create backdrops for many scenes, the filmmakers used a technique known as "matting." Images such as beautiful plantation mansions were painted on glass. The cinematographers would make one film of the glass and another film of the actors speaking their lines. The two films were then placed one on top of the other, and thus audiences would see Scarlett and Rhett against a beautiful sunset or outside a stately mansion.

Gone with the Wind took viewers on a romantic, 3½-hour journey through a tragic part of American history. Audiences loved every minute of it. The expectations for *Gone with the Wind* were so high that anything less than the biggest, most creative epic of its time would have seemed like a failure.

David O. Selznick went on to produce other great movies. Unhappy that he couldn't make a film to surpass *Gone with the Wind*, he stopped making movies in 1957. His last movie was *A Farewell to Arms*. David O. Selznick died in 1965, but his greatest triumph still lives on.

(1941)
CITIZEN KANE

b/w
dir Orson Welles
pro Orson Welles
sc Herman J. Mankiewicz
st Orson Welles (Charles Foster Kane), William Alland (Jerry Thompson), Dorothy Comingore (Susan Alexander), Everett Sloan (Mr. Bernstein), Joseph Cotten (Jedediah Leland)

Citizen Kane is often called the greatest American movie of all time. Film critics and audiences alike use *Citizen Kane* as a standard with which to judge other movies. Scholars still study everything about the movie—from the plot to the lighting to the camera angles. But above all, *Citizen Kane* is entertaining and great fun to watch!

Before he signed a contract with RKO Studios, director Orson Welles had been thrilling audiences for years with his Mercury Theater radio programs. On Halloween night in 1938, Welles broadcast a production of the classic H. G. Wells science fiction story, *The War of the Worlds*, about Martians invading Earth. The production was so realistic that many listeners believed Martians had really landed. Much of the nation was thrown into chaos.

Charles Foster Kane rules a newspaper empire.

Welles could spin a great tale, and he brought that talent to film. The story of Charles Foster Kane, the power-mad newspaper tycoon in *Citizen Kane*, is the kind of story that audiences loved.

The screenplay, written by Herman Mankiewicz, was based on the life of multimillionaire newspaper owner William Randolph Hearst. Americans have always been attracted to real-life stories of power, and Hearst's life provided the perfect plot for a movie. Mankiewicz got the idea for the script while working at one of Hearst's many newspapers.

Citizen Kane begins as Charles Foster Kane dies. Through newsreel footage, we learn about Kane's rise and fall. But newsreels do not tell the whole story. A reporter tries to discover the meaning of "Rosebud," Kane's last word before dying.

The Rosebud mystery is simply a clever way for Welles to tell the story of Kane's life. The movie is made up of a series of flashbacks—the memories of people who were close to Charles Foster Kane. Welles (who himself plays Kane) leads us on a winding road through the man's life. We learn how the people in Kane's life loved and hated him. Kane, we find out, never loved anyone but himself.

Citizen Kane is a great movie, in part, because it is fun to watch. Welles was a clever director who knew how audiences thought and knew how to appeal to them. The audience is let in on Kane's secrets. In fact, the viewers know more about Charles Foster Kane than the characters telling the story.

Welles's love for theater and magic show up in his filmmaking methods. The way he focused the camera, lit the set and characters, and cut to each shot showed things about his characters that words could not express. Some directors use the camera to impress the audience—just to show how good they are with lighting and angles. But Welles, filmmaker-magician, knew how to use the camera to make his story more dramatic, interesting, and fun.

"Mr. Kane is a man who got everything he wanted and then lost it."

It is a dark, gray day. Far up on a hill sits an immense, decaying mansion. An old man, Charles Foster Kane, lies on a bed inside the mansion. Kane utters the word "Rosebud" and dies.

We first learn about the life of Charles Foster Kane through a "News on the March!" newsreel. Kane's old mansion, called Xanadu, was once a grand and glorious estate with great works of art, 100,000 trees, and its own zoo.

Kane was one of the most powerful men in the world, the newsreel explains. Some thought he was a Communist, others thought he was a Fascist. Kane's own description of himself was: "I am, have been, and will be only one thing—an American."

He was accused of starting the Spanish-American War. He almost became governor of New York. By the time he died, Kane had fallen from power. The newsreel ends.

But the newsreel's producer does not think the footage tells the whole story. "When Charles Foster Kane died, he said just one word," the producer says. He orders a reporter, Jerry Thompson, to find out what Rosebud means.

Thompson tries to talk to Kane's second wife, Susan Alexander, a nightclub singer. Susan is down on her luck and a drunk. "Why don't you people just leave me alone," she tells Thompson.

Thompson goes to the Thatcher Memorial Library. Walter Thatcher was the banker who controlled Kane's money until

Mr. Thatcher tells young Charles he's going to be rich. Charles doesn't want to leave his home and family.

Kane was old enough to manage his own affairs. Thatcher's personal memoirs tell Kane's story from the beginning.

The story begins in 1871. Young Charles is playing with his sled in the snow outside his mother's boardinghouse. An old boarder has given Mrs. Kane the deed to a profitable gold mine. Mr. Thatcher's bank operates the mine and buys up more businesses with the profits. Charles will take control of the fortune when he turns 21. Charles is sent away to boarding school.

By the time Charles is 21, he is one of the richest men in the world. One of the businesses he owns is a small newspaper called the *New York Inquirer*.

With the help of his friends Mr. Bernstein and Jed Leland, Kane decides to run the paper himself. He angers Mr. Thatcher by using the newspaper to attack big business, slumlords, and government corruption. When the stock market crashes in 1929, Kane loses a great deal of money and is forced to give up the newspaper. Thatcher's memories about Kane end there, but Thompson has not learned about Rosebud.

Thompson goes to see Mr. Bernstein, who tells his own Kane story: Kane builds the *Inquirer* into the largest newspaper in New York City. He uses the paper to stir up hatred toward Spain, bringing the United States to the brink of war. Kane marries the niece of the president of the United States. He becomes very powerful. The marriage fails, and Kane's wife and son die in a car crash.

Bernstein's story does not answer the Rosebud mystery. Bernstein tells Thompson: "Maybe [Rosebud] was something he lost. Mr. Kane was a man who lost almost everything he had."

Thompson goes to see Jed Leland, who is now an old man living in a hospital. "He never believed in anything except Charlie Kane," Leland says. Jed tells his Kane story: Kane decides to run for governor. He meets a young woman, Susan Alexander, and they become friends. Kane spends a lot of time at her apartment.

Kane runs against Jim Gettys for the office of governor. Gettys exposes Kane's relationship with Susan Alexander in the newspapers, and Kane loses the election. Jed thinks that Kane is becoming too hungry for power. Jed takes a job at one of Kane's newspapers in Chicago, and he and Kane stop speaking.

Kane marries Susan Alexander. He helps her become an opera singer. He even builds an opera house in Chicago so Susan can sing there. Her debut is a failure. Jed Leland writes a bad review of Susan's performance, and Kane fires him.

Leland's story ends, but Thompson has not come any closer to finding out about Rosebud. He goes back to see

Susan Alexander, who finally agrees to talk. She tells him that her singing career was all Charles's idea. Susan did not even want to be an opera singer.

We flash back to Xanadu: Susan threatens to quit singing, but Charles orders her to continue. Susan tries to commit suicide. The marriage falls apart. Sick of Charles controlling everything about her life, Susan leaves him.

Susan finishes her story. She tells Thompson to go to Xanadu and find Raymond, the butler.

Raymond does not know what Rosebud means. He and Thompson walk through a huge room full of priceless statues, artwork, and antiques. Workers are sorting through Kane's possessions—cataloging the valuables and burning the trash. "I don't think any word can explain a man's life," Raymond says. "No, I guess Rosebud is just a piece in a jigsaw puzzle. A missing piece."

A worker picks up an old sled, the one that Kane played with as a boy, and throws it into a fire with some garbage. As the fire consumes the sled, a word painted on it slowly fades away. The word is "Rosebud."

ORSON WELLES, BOY GENIUS

Orson Welles was only in his mid-20s when RKO Studios hired him to make movies. He was best known at the time for his work in theater and radio. Welles's acting company, the Mercury Theater, not only performed the infamous broadcast of *The War of the Worlds* but also dramatized classic stories like *Heart of Darkness*. Many Mercury Theater actors and writers went with Welles to Hollywood.

RKO's offer to Welles was unique. The movie studio gave him something very few Hollywood directors had, especially one as young and untested as Welles: complete control over the artistic aspects of his films.

But Welles was an outsider in Hollywood. Many people were jealous of his talent and the fact that he had so much artistic freedom. And his ego was as big as Kane's.

In fact, Welles's ego caused a controversy about who actually wrote *Citizen Kane*. Even though Herman Mankiewicz wrote the script, Welles insisted on taking credit as cowriter. Everything Welles did—be it acting, writing, or directing—was considered the work of a genius. Why he wanted to take praise for work he didn't do is unknown.

Before he came to Hollywood, Orson Welles thrilled audiences with his radio dramas.

The fact that *Citizen Kane* was critical of the powerful William Randolph Hearst did not make Welles any more loved in Hollywood. The movie industry paid the rebel genius back by nearly snubbing him during the Academy Awards ceremony. (Mankiewicz and Welles did win the award for Best Screenplay, even though Welles wrote very little of it.)

Welles's next film, *The Magnificent Ambersons*, is considered by some critics to be nearly as good as *Citizen Kane*. But while Welles was out of the country, the studio cut much of the ending of the film without his knowledge. *The Magnificent Ambersons* does not make much sense at the end. By all reports, if the movie had been left untouched, it would have been as great as *Citizen Kane*.

Welles had lost his stature and, worse, his artistic control at the studio. He became frustrated and only made a few more feature films. His last Hollywood movie was *Touch of Evil* (1958), which is considered brilliant.

Near the end of his life, Orson Welles had lost a lot of respect. Critics like to think that there are two Orson Welles: the genius who created *Citizen Kane* and the clown magician who could be seen doing card tricks with Johnny Carson on the "Tonight Show." But despite his fall from fame, nothing can change the fact that Orson Welles, at the age of 25, made one of the greatest movies ever.

THE MANCHURIAN CANDIDATE

(1962)

b/w
dir John Frankenheimer
pro George Axelrod and John Frankenheimer
sc George Axelrod
st Frank Sinatra (Bennett Marco), Laurence Harvey (Raymond Shaw), Angela Lansbury (Mother), James Gregory (John Iselin), Henry Silva (Chunjim), Leslie Parrish (Jocie Jordon), John McGiver (Thomas Jordon)

Over the years, audiences have fallen in love with the secret agents of the spy movies. Movies that feature super-spies, like the dashing James Bond, are full of action, suspense, and villains.

Secret-agent movies are entertaining. But other kinds of spy movies are just as interesting. Political thrillers go beyond the super-spy formula to explore the dark, secret side of politics and government.

Filmmakers and filmgoers have been interested in the secret side of politics for many years. Political thrillers became popular in the 1950s, when the Cold War between the United States and the Soviet Union was fought by the secret government agencies of each country.

The best political thrillers take a realistic look at government. *Three Days of the Condor* (1975) stars Robert Redford as a Central Intelligence Agency (CIA) analyst who is hunted by the CIA itself. The movie raised many doubts and suspicions about the American government. Audiences were just as amazed as Redford's character that the CIA might be able to operate without having to answer to the American people.

Seven Days in May (1964) is a classic movie that takes a frightening look at how easy it is to abuse power. Burt Lancaster plays an American general who plots to overthrow the president. The plot would have succeeded had not the general's assistant, played by Kirk Douglas, convinced the president of the impending danger. The movie shocked audiences by showing that a real military takeover was possible.

One reason *Seven Days in May* is so good is that the director, John Frankenheimer, knew how to make realistic but suspenseful political thrillers. Two years earlier, Frankenheimer had made what is considered the best political thriller of all time, *The Manchurian Candidate*. The movie, based on a 1959 book by Richard Condon, tells the story of a plot to put a Communist agent in the White House.

Laurence Harvey plays American Raymond Shaw, a Korean War veteran who has been brainwashed by Communists. Raymond's mother is a Communist secret agent married to a dim-witted anti-Communist senator. Mother orders Raymond to assassinate the presidential nominee. Only Bennett Marco, Raymond's commanding officer (played by Frank Sinatra), is able to stop the assassination plot.

The Manchurian Candidate is considered a classic for many reasons. The performances of Harvey and Sinatra are brilliant. Angela Lansbury won an Oscar for her portrayal of the power-hungry mother. The scene in which

Mother gives Raymond instructions to kill the presidential nominee is one of the greatest moments in movie history.

George Axelrod, who wrote the screenplay, took the outrageous wit of Condon's novel and gave it a dark edge. Frankenheimer's pacing of Axelrod's scenes adds to the suspense.

Frankenheimer and Axelrod use a surreal dream scene to tell both Ben and the audience about the Communist plot to take over the American government. Ben dreams that Communist scientists are displaying brainwashed American soldiers to a group of Communist agents. The soldiers think they are attending a garden club meeting made up of American women.

The dream scene is one of the most innovative in movie history. As the camera circles the room, we feel like we are on a merry-go-round. Every time we go around, we see either a room filled with Communist agents or—from the perspective of the brainwashed American soldiers—filled with elderly women.

To create the scene, Frankenheimer had to film it from many different perspectives and from a number of different angles. Filming the scene took seven days. The scene moves in and out of Ben's mind with such ease that viewers don't realize how complicated the scene was to shoot. The dream sequence in *The Manchurian Candidate* shows us that great moviemakers are not afraid to take creative risks.

"Why don't you pass the time by playing a little solitaire."
A U.S. Army squad led by Raymond Shaw and Ben Marco is out on patrol in Korea in 1952. Chunjim, a Korean guide, is with them. As the men walk along a ridge, they are ambushed by a group of Soviet soldiers. The Americans are all knocked unconscious. The leader of the Soviets

walks up to Chunjim and shakes his hand. The Americans are flown away by Soviet helicopters.

When the Korean War ends, Raymond returns to the United States a hero. He has won a medal for saving his patrol from an enemy attack. In Washington, D.C., Raymond is greeted at the airport by a military band and scores of admirers and reporters. Raymond is annoyed by all the attention.

Raymond is also welcomed by his mother and stepfather, Senator Johnny Iselin. Johnny, a rabid anti-Communist, is using his stepson's heroism to gain popularity with the voters. Raymond hates his mother and stepfather for their selfish ambition.

Bennett Marco becomes a major in Washington, D.C. Every night he has the same nightmare. He dreams his patrol is sitting with a bunch of old women in a hotel lobby. The women keep changing into Communist soldiers and back again. Chunjim is there too.

One of the Communists, a Chinese man named Yen Lo, explains that the American soldiers think they are at a garden club meeting. The patrol has been captured and brainwashed, he explains. The Communists plan to send the soldiers back to the United States as heroes. Raymond has been brainwashed into acting as an assassin for the Communists.

Ben tells the army about his dream. Army intelligence does not believe the dream is true. In New York, Ben confronts Raymond, who tells him that another member of the patrol has had the same dream. Army officials finally believe Ben. They have him follow Raymond to find out who the secret agents are and what the Communists want Raymond to do.

Raymond's phone rings. The person on the phone asks

In *The Manchurian Candidate*'s famous dream scene, Ben Marco (left) and Raymond Shaw (center) believe they are at a garden club meeting.

Raymond to play a game of solitaire, and Raymond pulls out a deck of cards. The queen of diamonds comes up, and Raymond stops playing. The queen of diamonds is the symbol that the Communists use to control Raymond's mind.

Raymond marries Jocie, the daughter of Senator Thomas Jordan, Johnny and Mother's political enemy. On his honeymoon, Raymond sees Johnny on TV attacking Senator Jordan.

Raymond rushes to Mother's house and argues with her about Johnny. Mother, who is actually a Communist agent, grabs a deck of cards. She pulls out the queen of diamonds, which puts Raymond in a trance. Mother tells Raymond there is something he must do for her.

Mother orders Raymond to kill Senator Jordan. After Raymond shoots the Senator, Jocie comes downstairs to find her father dead and Raymond standing over him. Raymond kills Jocie too. Even though the police do not suspect

43

If Mother's scheme succeeds, Johnny Iselin will become president of the United States.

Raymond, Ben knows that Raymond has killed Jocie and her father.

Ben gets a phone call from Raymond. He is now at a hotel across the street from Madison Square Garden, where Johnny Iselin is about to be nominated for vice-president. Ben enters Raymond's hotel room and finds him lying in a chair. He is crying. "Who killed Jocie, Ben?" he asks. "Tell me, I've got to know."

Ben pulls out a deck of cards. Raymond turns over one card and sees the red queen. With Raymond's mind under his control, Ben is able to get all the answers from Raymond about what really happened in Korea.

The phone rings. Raymond listens for a while and, to Ben's surprise, says, "Yes. I understand, Mother." Raymond goes to see Mother, who tells him to kill the presidential nominee. With him dead, the inept Johnny Iselin is poised to become the next president. But Mother, as First Lady, will really be in power.

Ben rushes to Madison Square Garden. He thinks he's too late to stop the assassination. Raymond is indeed going to shoot someone—but not the presidential nominee. Just before Ben reaches Raymond, Mother and Johnny lie dead on the podium.

"You couldn't have stopped them," Raymond says to Ben. "The army couldn't have stopped them. So I had to." He puts the rifle up to his head and pulls the trigger.

POLITICS AND MOVIES

The Manchurian Candidate shows how the camera, the screenplay, and the actors all work together to create a masterpiece. When a movie as great as *The Manchurian Candidate* also gives a strong message about the real world, it is destined to be a classic.

During the Cold War of the 1950s and early 1960s, Americans lived in fear of Communism. *The Manchurian Candidate* had the same kind of paranoid mood. When the movie came out, both Communists and anti-Communists thought the movie criticized them unfairly. These people did not understand the movie's point—that the Cold War was traumatic for everyone.

Like *Citizen Kane*, *The Manchurian Candidate* did not get a great reception when it was first released. Many viewers thought the movie was bizarre and not very realistic. But *The Manchurian Candidate* was much closer to historical fact than most people realized.

The anti-Communist senator in *The Manchurian Candidate* was based on a real senator, Joseph McCarthy, who brought many suspected Communists to trial in the 1950s. In addition, a year after *The Manchurian Candidate* was released, President John F. Kennedy was assassinated.

After Kennedy's assassination, Frank Sinatra (who had been friends with the president) refused to let the movie be shown again until the 1980s. He used his influence to have the movie pulled from circulation. Why did this star suddenly decide that a great movie should not be shown? No one knows for sure.

Some people think the film was pulled simply because Frankenheimer and Axelrod had a fight with the movie studio. Another popular story is that Frank Sinatra felt that the assassination scene in the movie stirred up disturbing memories of President Kennedy's assassination.

The Cold War, the anti-Communist witchhunts of the 1950s, and the assassination of President Kennedy were indeed traumatic events in American history. *The Manchurian Candidate* dealt with issues that brought up many painful feelings for the American public.

Johnny's crusade against Communists recalled Senator Joseph McCarthy and the "Red Scare" of the 1950s.

Frank Sinatra finally allowed *The Manchurian Candidate* to be shown again commercially in 1987—to promote the movie's release on video. Movie critics and audiences, many of whom never had a chance to see the movie when it first came out, flocked to see it.

Classic movies must stand the test of time. Unlike most classics, however, *The Manchurian Candidate* stood that test while hidden away. As George Axelrod said about the unique history of *The Manchurian Candidate:* "It went from failure to classic without ever passing through success."

Nothing tops *Psycho*'s classic shower scene, featuring Janet Leigh.

(1960)
PSYCHO

b/w
dir Alfred Hitchcock
pro Alfred Hitchcock
sc Joseph Stefano
st Janet Leigh (Marion Crane), Anthony Perkins (Norman Bates), John Gavin (Sam Loomis), Vera Miles (Lila Crane), Martin Balsam (Milton Arbogast)

What happens when one of the greatest directors of all time makes a movie about a nice young man who dresses up like his dead mother and kills people? Audiences found out in 1960, when the king of the suspense thriller, Alfred Hitchcock, made a movie based on Robert Bloch's novel, *Psycho*. The result is still considered the greatest horror movie of all time—more than 30 years after it first struck fear into the hearts of moviegoers.

By 1960 Hitchcock was quite famous. For 25 years he had been directing suspense thrillers. Movies like *Rebecca* (1940), *Shadow of a Doubt* (1943), and *Rear Window* (1954) are just a few of the artful and entertaining Hitchcock masterpieces that kept audiences on the edges of their seats and kept critics analyzing every frame of film.

Hitchcock movies always look beneath the surface to find the real story. There is always something going on behind a closed door. There is always a killer lurking behind a sweet smile.

Psycho is about a young man named Norman Bates who runs a family motel. Norman thinks his dead mother is still alive. She is alive—in a way. Norman has taken on her identity. Norman is a shy, polite man. But when he turns into his mother, he kills anyone who intrudes on their own little world.

The movie takes us on a trip into the dark, twisted mind of someone who looks like the boy next door. There are no monsters in *Psycho*, only a tortured young man with a split personality. Bloch got the idea for his book from a real-life psychotic, Ed Gein, who wore the skin of his dead mother and killed people.

What puts *Psycho* far above the normal horror movie? For one thing, the acting is excellent—especially the performance by Anthony Perkins as the cursed Norman Bates.

But the genius of Alfred Hitchcock really makes *Psycho* a classic. Hitchcock shows his talent in *Psycho*'s shower scene—the most famous horror scene in movie history. Hitchcock used 70 different camera angles to show Norman, under the control of his dead mother, kill the character Marion, played by Janet Leigh. The chaotic use of the camera, combined with the frightening music of Bernard Herrmann's soundtrack, turned the simple task of taking a shower into a terrifying experience for millions of moviegoers.

Like all great directors, Hitchcock had the ability to craft complex movies without taking away from the excitement of watching them. His use of camera angles, lighting, and action in *Psycho* was carefully designed to take moviegoers to new levels of suspense and fear.

On the set of *Psycho*: Alfred Hitchcock — the master of suspense and terror — with Anthony Perkins (right)

"She might have fooled me but she didn't fool Mother."

Sam and Marion are in a dingy downtown hotel in Phoenix, Arizona. They are having an affair. Marion asks Sam to marry her. But Sam doesn't want to get married until he can clear up his money problems.

When Marion goes to her job at a real estate agency, she sees an opportunity. A rich oil tycoon, Tom Cassidy, is buying a house with $40,000 in cash. Not wanting the cash in the office, Marion's boss asks her to take the money to the bank on her way home.

But Marion does not go to the bank. She packs a bag and drives out of town, imagining how happy Sam will be when she greets him with $40,000.

In the morning, a cop questions Marion, who has spent the night in her car. Marion fears that she will be followed

Stealing Mr. Cassidy's money will only lead Marion to more trouble.

and goes to a used-car lot to exchange cars. The cop is suspicious, but does nothing.

Feeling guilty, Marion imagines Mr. Cassidy's voice: "I'll track her, never you doubt it!" Through a violent rainstorm, Marion spots a sign saying Bates Motel. She pulls up to the motel but finds no one in the office. Marion sees a large old house up on a hill. The house is dark, except for a light in one room. A lone figure walks past the window.

A thin young man, Norman Bates, comes running down the stairs from the house. Marion asks if he has a vacancy. The rooms are always vacant, Normans explains, because the new highway no longer brings travelers past the motel.

Norman gives Marion cabin 1 and asks her to the house for dinner. She agrees, but first she goes to the cabin and hides her money inside a newspaper. Suddenly, an old woman's voice pierces the air: "No, I tell you. No! I won't have you bringing strange young girls in here for supper!" Norman comes back down from the house with some food and explains to Marion that his mother "isn't quite herself today."

They go into the back parlor of the office to eat. Norman seems agitated when he talks about his mother. Marion decides that she should return the stolen money. She goes back to her cabin. She is taking a shower when, suddenly, the shower curtain is torn open.

Marion turns around to see an old woman with a large knife raised over her head. Marion screams as the knife is plunged into her body again and again.

Norman is shouting at his mother for what she has done. He comes rushing into the cabin and wraps Marion's body in the shower curtain. He cleans up the cabin, covering any trace that Marion has been there. He puts Marion's body and her possessions, including the newspaper that hides the money, into her car. Then he dumps the car into a murky pond.

Fifteen miles away in Fairvale, Sam is working in his hardware store. Marion's sister, Lila, has come looking for Marion.

Marion's boss wants to find her too. He has hired a detective, Milton Arbogast, to find Marion and the stolen money. Arbogast comes to the hardware store and questions Sam and Lila. All three are stumped about Marion's disappearance.

Arbogast drives to the Bates Motel and questions Norman. Norman tries to convince Arbogast that Marion left the morning after her stay, but Arbogast is suspicious. He walks to the house on the hill and is killed by the same old woman who killed Marion.

When Arbogast doesn't return from the motel, Sam drives there himself. He spies an old woman in the window of the house.

Sam and Lila visit the town's sheriff, Al Chambers. Sam tells Chambers that Arbogast went to question Mrs. Bates at the motel and didn't return. To Sam's surprise, Al says that Mrs. Bates is dead. She killed her boyfriend and then committed suicide ten years before, he explains.

At the Bates house, Norman wants to hide his mother. He carries her down to the fruit cellar. Sam and Lila arrive at the motel, and Lila finds evidence that Marion was in cabin 1. While Sam distracts Norman, Lila searches the house.

Norman wonders where Lila is. He hits Sam on the head with a teapot and knocks him out. Seeing Norman, Lila runs down to the fruit cellar to hide.

The cellar is dreary and dark. An old woman, her back turned to Lila, sits in a rocking chair in the middle of the

Lila finds the real Mrs. Bates and recoils in horror.

room. Lila walks up to the woman and touches her shoulder. The chair turns. The old woman is dead—her skeleton covered only by a wrinkled layer of skin. Lila screams and another old woman comes through the door, holding the knife that killed Arbogast and Marion.

Sam comes up behind the old woman and they struggle. Her wig comes off to reveal that she is really Norman.

At the police station, a psychiatrist explains that Norman killed his mother and her lover out of jealousy. Now Norman's mother has taken over his personality, killing anyone who would come between them. In the last scene, we see Norman sitting alone in a room. Mother is in complete control.

CLASSIC HORROR MOVIES

What makes the horror movie different from any other type of movie? For one thing, the star of the movie usually spends his, her, or its time trying to kill or maim everyone else.

The characters in classic horror films become a part of movie legend. Thanks to Anthony Perkins, Norman Bates has become the classic "psycho."

Most of the classic horror characters are not human. But they have become famous, in part, because of the humans who played them. Boris Karloff made the Monster famous in the original *Frankenstein*. That movie came out in 1931, and it can still bring nightmares to even the most cynical viewer.

But characters alone do not turn a horror movie into a classic. The story is as important as the star. *Frankenstein* is based on a novel by Mary Shelley, a story that was written long before movies were invented. *Dracula* was created in the mind of novelist Bram Stoker. His book was published in 1897.

Robert Louis Stevenson got the idea for his classic novel *The Strange Case of Dr. Jekyll and Mr. Hyde* from a nightmare. The evil Mr. Hyde takes over the nice Dr. Jekyll's mind, much like Norman's mother takes over his mind. Three versions of the movie were made—in 1920, 1932, and 1941. Each one was just as frightening as the book.

When horror movies take frightening ideas and make them just as scary on screen, the nightmares of the writers become our own. These are the horror movies that deserve to be called classics.

Opposite: Boris Karloff as the Monster

(1977)

THE GODFATHER EPIC

color
dir Francis Ford Coppola
pro Albert S. Ruddy (Part I); Francis Ford Coppola, Gary Frederickson, Fred Roos (Part II)
sc Mario Puzo, Francis Ford Coppola
st Marlon Brando (Vito Corleone), Al Pacino (Michael Corleone), James Caan (Sonny Corleone), Robert Duvall (Tom Hagen), Diane Keaton (Kay Adams) Talia Shire (Connie Rizzi), Gianni Russo (Carlo Rizzi), John Cazale (Fredo Corleone), Robert De Niro (young Vito Corleone)

The *Godfather Epic* is actually two movies: *The Godfather* (1972) and *The Godfather Part II* (1974). Director/screenwriter Francis Ford Coppola and screenwriter Mario Puzo based the Godfather movies on Puzo's novel, *The Godfather*.

In *The Godfather Epic*, we follow two generations of the Corleone family, members of the Mafia, who deal in illegal businesses like gambling, drug trafficking, and prostitution. But *The Godfather Epic* is more than a typical gangster movie. It is based on true historical events and actual Mafia families. The movie takes a realistic look at the rules and code of ethics inside the Mafia. *The Godfather Epic* explores themes that are important to most of us: family ties, ethnic pride, and honor.

The epic stretches from the turn of the century through the 1960s. Many Americans saw their own family history in the godfather movies, because the head of the Corleone family, Vito Corleone, immigrates to the United States in search of the American Dream. But the violent way the Corleones try to realize that dream ends up destroying the family.

Vito Corleone escapes the terror of the Mafia in his native Sicily and comes to America with millions of other immigrants who seek a better life. Vito may be a criminal, but his family is more important to him than his business.

Vito's youngest son, Michael, is more ambitious and ruthless than his father. He tries to carry on the tradition of the Corleone family, but his greed leaves him lonely and isolated. Michael's downfall is a sad ending to a great family saga.

Audiences and critics appreciated the way Coppola put this story on the screen. The lighting, sets, and pace of the movie turned it into an emotional experience for moviegoers. Coppola decided to film on location in Sicily, to cast Marlon Brando as Vito Corleone, and to cast Al Pacino as Michael. Paramount Pictures was against all these ideas, but Coppola would not back down.

As important as Coppola's talent and vision were, much of the credit for making *The Godfather Epic* a classic must go to the actors. Marlon Brando won an Oscar for Best Actor in Part I. He came out of retirement to play the role of Vito Corleone, and most critics say it is his best performance ever.

The *Godfather* movies made stars of Al Pacino, Robert De Niro, Robert Duvall, James Caan, and Diane Keaton. Pacino, playing Michael, did a remarkable job changing his character from the nice young son in *The Godfather* to

The creative genius behind *The Godfather Epic*: **Francis Ford Coppola**

the ruthless head of the family in *The Godfather Part II*. Robert De Niro's performance as young Vito Corleone in Part II even made some people forget Marlon Brando's Oscar-winning performance as the older Vito.

Both movies won Oscars for Best Picture—the only time both a movie and its sequel have done so. Francis Ford Coppola won an Oscar for Best Director for Part II.

Part I, *The Godfather*, tells the story of Vito as an older man who is preparing to leave the family business to his sons. *The Godfather Part II* tells the story of young Vito as he starts his family and Michael as he almost destroys it.

In 1977 Coppola combined the two movies and reedited them in chronological order. He also added some scenes that had been cut out of the original releases. The result is *The Godfather Epic*. Whether you watch the movies separately or together, *The Godfather* films are an amazing experience.

"I'm gonna make him an offer he can't refuse."

In Corleone, Sicily, in 1901, nine-year-old Vito Andolini's father, mother, and older brother are murdered by the head of the local Mafia, Don Ciccio. Vito escapes Sicily and ends up in New York City. An immigration official renames him Vito Corleone.

Sixteen years later, Vito is married and living in the Little Italy section of New York City. He has four children.

Vito and two friends, Clemenza and Tessio, run a small crime operation. Don Fanutti, the local crime boss, tries to take money from them. Vito kills Don Fanutti and becomes the most feared and respected crime boss in Little Italy.

Years later Vito's hair is gray and his jowls sag. He is one of the most powerful organized crime figures in the United States. His children—Sonny, Fredo, Michael, and Connie—are now adults. Clemenza and Tessio are still Vito's closest and most trusted associates. Vito's adopted son, Tom Hagen, serves as Vito's legal advisor.

A famous singer, Johnny Fontane, wants a part in an important movie. But the producer does not want to give Johnny the part. Johnny goes to Vito for help. "I'm gonna make him an offer he can't refuse," Vito tells Johnny.

Top: Young Vito Corleone (Robert De Niro) kills Don Fanutti. Bottom: Marlon Brando (second from left) played the aging Vito, surrounded by his sons Michael, Sonny, and Fredo.

Tom Hagen goes to Hollywood to persuade the producer to hire Johnny. The producer explains to Tom that Johnny stole a girlfriend from him. The next morning, the producer wakes up and finds the severed head of his prized horse in his bed. Johnny gets the part.

Vito is gunned down by men from a rival crime family, the Tattaglia family, while shopping at the outdoor market in Little Italy. Vito survives the attack.

Michael Corleone, a World War II hero who once wanted nothing to do with the family business, wants revenge for the attack on his father. Michael arranges a meeting with Solozzo, a Tattaglia associate, and McCluskey, a crooked cop. Michael kills them both. He hides out in Sicily to escape retaliation from the Tattaglias.

In Sicily, Michael meets a young woman, Apollonia, and marries her. Someone tries to kill Michael, but Apollonia is killed instead.

Meanwhile, in New York, Sonny Corleone is set up by Connie's husband, Carlo Rizzi, and is murdered. Vito calls a meeting of the heads of the five major crime families. He asks the men to stop the killing. After the meeting, Vito tells Tom that the Barzini family killed Sonny.

Michael comes home from Sicily and takes over the family business. He marries his old girlfriend, Kay Adams, and decides to invest in gambling casinos in Nevada.

Back in New York, Michael seeks out his father for advice. Vito says that Barzini will try to assassinate Michael at a meeting. Vito tells his son: "Whoever comes to you with this Barzini meeting, he's the traitor." Vito dies of a heart attack.

At Vito's funeral, Tessio tells Michael that he can set up a meeting with Barzini. Tom says, "I always thought [the traitor] would be Clemenza, not Tessio."

Michael takes revenge for his brother's death by killing Tessio and Carlo. He then kills Barzini and other crime family heads. In Lake Tahoe, Nevada, while Michael and Kay are getting ready for bed, someone tries to assassinate Michael.

Michael wants to move his crime operation into Cuba with Hyman Roth, one of his father's old business partners. On a trip to Cuba, Michael realizes that Roth was the one who tried to kill him in Lake Tahoe and that his brother Fredo had him set up to be killed.

At a New Year's Eve party in Havana, Michael grabs Fredo and kisses him on the lips. "I know it was you, Fredo," Michael tells him. "You broke my heart." Fredo runs from his brother.

Meanwhile, Michael tries to have Hyman Roth killed. Roth is injured but he survives.

In Nevada Michael asks his mother if he is doing the wrong thing by alienating his family. You can never lose your family, she answers. "Times are changing," Michael tells her.

Fredo comes home to Nevada. "I don't want anything to happen to him," Michael tells one of his men, "while my mother's alive." Kay is fed up with the crime business and she leaves Michael. Mama Corleone dies.

Michael still wants to kill Hyman Roth, who has since retired and moved to Israel. Tom disagrees, saying there is no need to kill Roth—they have already put him out of business. Tom asks Michael if he wants to wipe everyone out. "Only my enemies," Michael says.

Kay comes home to visit her kids, but Michael slams the door in her face. He orders his men to kill Fredo and Hyman Roth. Michael sits alone in his study, having lost everyone he loves.

MOVIES AND GANGSTERS

During the 1920s and 1930s, many businesses in the United States were controlled by organized crime. Gangsters, like the legendary Al Capone, were violent criminals. They lived by their own rules and their own code of ethics. Loyalty was rewarded with power and riches. Breaking the rules meant certain death.

Law-abiding citizens lived in fear of the gangsters. But many people were fascinated by the dangerous—and wealthy—criminals. After all, during the Great Depression of the 1930s, few people could make money the legal way.

In 1930, when Edward G. Robinson played the Caponelike character Rico in *Little Caesar*, audiences and critics began the same love/hate relationship with gangster movies as they had with the criminals themselves. When James Cagney hit the screen in *The Public Enemy* (1931), America's love affair with gangster movies kicked into high gear.

Cagney was the first actor to make the audience identify with a gangster. He played Tom Powers, an energetic, wisecracking young outlaw. Like everyone else, Tom needs love and family. Eventually, he wants to leave his life of crime and make peace with his family.

Tom Powers was the first in a long line of movie "antiheroes"—characters that we cheer for even though they are the "bad guys." People sometimes criticize gangster movies for making heroes out of criminals. But in many gangster movies, the "good guys"—like the police, judges, and politicians—turn out to be more corrupt than the crooks.

The movie *Bonnie and Clyde* is based on real-life bank robbers Bonnie Parker and Clyde Barrow. Like many gangsters, Parker and Barrow were folk heroes. They robbed banks during the Depression, when most people were poor and when bankers were seen as evil and greedy.

In addition to telling us about life in the 1930s, *Bonnie and Clyde*, like all great films, says something about the world at the time the movie was made. *Bonnie and Clyde* was released in 1967. During the 1960s, many young people did not respect authority. Young rebels all across the United States could identify with Bonnie and Clyde. The characters quickly became heroes to a whole generation.

Why are audiences so fascinated by gangster movies? Maybe we envy the gangster's power and money. Or maybe the gangster movie touches the rebellious side of all of us.

Bonnie and Clyde were folk heroes during the 1930s. In the rebellious 1960s, Faye Dunaway (second from right) and Warren Beatty (center) made the outlaws famous once again.

Woody Allen and Diane Keaton make us laugh and cry in *Annie Hall*.

(1977)

ANNIE HALL

color
dir Woody Allen
pro Charles H. Joffe
sc Woody Allen and Marshall Brickman
st Woody Allen (Alvy Singer), Diane Keaton (Annie Hall), Tony Roberts (Rob)

Annie Hall is about the relationship between a comedian, Alvy Singer (Woody Allen), and a singer, Annie Hall (Diane Keaton). The movie takes a humorous and personal look at everything from politics to religion to sex. One reason *Annie Hall* is such an enjoyable movie is that the audience can relate to Annie and Alvy's hang-ups.

The genius behind *Annie Hall* is writer, actor, and director Woody Allen. With *Annie Hall*, Allen stretched the limits of filmmaking. In some scenes, Alvy talks directly to the audience. In other scenes, total strangers walk up to Alvy on the street and give him their opinions. Sometimes characters from the past and the present are mixed on the same frame.

Annie Hall won a number of Oscars, including Best

Woody Allen usually plays a nervous, insecure person who helps us laugh at our own fears.

Picture, Best Director for Woody Allen, Best Actress for Diane Keaton, and Best Screenplay for Allen and Marshall Brickman.

Annie Hall is referred to as a "serious comedy"—a movie that uses humor to tell a dramatic story. Woody Allen made serious comedy popular with audiences, and his brand of humor influenced other comic filmmakers like Rob Reiner (*When Harry Met Sally*) and Albert Brooks (*Defending Your Life*).

Annie Hall might be the best serious comedy of all time. But Woody Allen is quick to count the early classic comedies as big influences on his movies. Even during the silent-movie era, when comedies featured plenty of slapstick humor, some comedies made audiences both laugh and cry.

The movie comedy was born during the first decade of this century with the great filmmaker D. W. Griffith. His comedies entertained audiences with crazy car chases and hilarious pratfalls.

The Keystone comedies, which included the popular Keystone Kops movies, began in 1912. The Keystone comedies also used amazing stunts and wild car chases to keep audiences laughing and on the edge of their seats.

The early comedies were fun to watch. But there were two pioneer filmmakers who felt that comedies could also tell meaningful stories. One of these filmmakers was Buster Keaton.

Actor/director Buster Keaton could make the most death-defying stunts look easy. He also knew how to use comedy to tell an emotional story. Keaton's *The General* (1927), for instance, is about a young man who tries to prove his worth during the Civil War. Audiences were thrilled by the famous runaway train scene in *The General*. But the stunt was also a way to put across the movie's message—that individual will and strength can overcome adversity.

Only one other filmmaker could rival Keaton's comic genius. While Keaton relied on death-defying stunts to put his messages across, Charlie Chaplin moved audiences with charming, funny, and tragic stories.

Chaplin used silent film to its full potential. His characters could tell an entire story with a simple look, a bowed head, or a wide smile. Like Buster Keaton, Charlie Chaplin starred in his own movies. His most famous character, "the Little Tramp," only had to wave his arms, wriggle his mustache, or waddle away to make audiences feel sorry for him.

In *Modern Times* (1936), Charlie Chaplin uses humor to take a stand against industry and big business.

Chaplin released *The Tramp* in 1915. At the beginning of the movie, the Little Tramp is homeless and poor. A car nearly knocks him over and covers him with dust. Audiences laughed. But at the same time, they realized how the "haves" look down on the "have-nots." Chaplin's movies were the first comedies to give important political and social messages—without any dialogue! The Little Tramp quickly became a hero all over the world.

The Great Depression affected all Americans—rich and poor—and the comedies of that time reflect the country's mood. The Marx brothers were popular comedians of the 1930s and 1940s. Their movies, like *Duck Soup* and *Horse Feathers*, used fast-paced, wacky humor to poke fun at rich snobs who looked down on the common people.

The economy improved during the 1940s and 1950s, and movie comedies reflected America's new optimism. Stars like Dean Martin, Jerry Lewis, Doris Day, and Tony Curtis made films that were uplifting and lighthearted, but lacking in political or social importance.

By the 1960s, movies reflected new attitudes about politics and war. Comedies were no different. In 1964 Stanley Kubrick made the classic comedy *Dr. Strangelove, or How I Learned to Stop Worrying and Love the Bomb.* The movie tells the story of an American bomber crew that accidentally drops an atomic bomb on Russia—thereby starting World War III. The subject of the movie was depressing. But *Dr. Strangelove* used humor and irony to speak to the fears of the Cold-War generation.

M*A*S*H (1970) is another classic comedy about war. The wisecracking Hawkeye Pierce, an American military doctor stationed in Korea during the Korean War, uses humor to fight both the horror of war and his frustration with military bureaucracy. The movie was a hit with young people who opposed the Vietnam War in the late 1960s and early 1970s.

Many critics think that comedies are too lighthearted to be called classics. But we need only look to Buster Keaton, Charlie Chaplin, and Woody Allen to see how wrong these critics are. A movie that makes us laugh can move us just as much—sometimes even more—than a serious film.

"I would never want to belong to a club that would have someone like me as a member."

Alvy Singer is a lovable, neurotic man with no self-confidence. He and his girlfriend, Annie Hall, have just broken up. He cannot figure out why.

To learn about Annie and Alvy's relationship, we have to learn a little bit about Annie and Alvy. We travel back to Alvy's childhood home in Brooklyn, New York, during World War II. Young Alvy is depressed because the universe is expanding. "If it's expanding, someday it will break apart, and that will be the end of everything," he says.

Alvy grows up to be a successful comedian and writer. But he is still as neurotic as when he was a kid. One day he and Annie are walking down the beach. They talk about their old relationships.

Alvy and Annie's previous affairs were messed up. We see Annie at a party a year before: She is with her old boyfriend, an arrogant actor who cons Annie into thinking he's really deep. The present-day Alvy and Annie are also at the party, standing in a corner. "Is he kidding with that stuff?" Alvy asks Annie. "C'mon, I was younger," Annie tells him.

The two lovers also remember when they first met: Alvy meets Annie through a mutual friend, Rob. They fall in love. At first everything is great, but then Alvy accuses Annie of having an affair. Annie is sick of Alvy's paranoia and she leaves him.

Alvy walks up to various people on the street and asks them about their love lives. He even asks a horse for an opinion.

Then Alvy appears as a cartoon character. Annie is the Wicked Queen from the fairy tale "Snow White." A cartoon Rob appears and tells Alvy to forget about Annie.

Soon, however, Annie and Alvy get back together. Alvy and Rob take Annie to the apartment where Alvy grew up. As they stand there, Alvy's memories come to life. We see all the weird characters from Alvy's past as they looked right after World War II. Alvy tries to talk to one of his relatives. "They can't hear you," Rob tells him.

Annie and Alvy are very different. Alvy is Jewish, and Annie is Christian. Alvy is scared of anything new and different. Annie likes to meet new people and try new things.

The couple goes to Los Angeles, where Alvy is supposed to present an entertainment award. But he hates the city

The bittersweet relationship between Annie Hall and Alvy Singer reminds moviegoers how hard it is to find true love.

so much he gets sick. Meanwhile, Annie is offered the chance to make a record with a famous L.A. producer.

Back in New York, Annie and Alvy break up again. Annie moves to Los Angeles; Alvy flies to L.A. to try and get her back. They meet at a restaurant. "Do you like living out here?" Alvy asks. "It's like living in Munchkinland."

Annie tells him that she is finally meeting people and having fun. She tells Alvy that his inability to enjoy life depresses her. Alvy gets into his car and proceeds to crash into every other car in the parking lot.

Annie and Alvy do not see each other for a long time. Finally, Annie moves back to New York, and they agree to be friends. To Alvy, being with Annie was an interesting experience that taught him a lot about himself and other people. The movie ends with Alvy writing a play about his relationship with Annie Hall.

WOODY ALLEN: MODERN COMIC GENIUS

Woody Allen was born Allan Konigsberg on December 1, 1935. His father worked in nightclubs in Manhattan, where Allen saw the stand-up comics who inspired his career.

Allen soon made a name for himself doing stand-up comedy. He was very nervous on stage. But his stuttering and his self-mocking personal stories made him a popular performer with whom audiences could sympathize.

Allen's real talent, though, was writing. He wrote constantly. In 1965 Allen wrote the screenplay for the movie *What's New, Pussycat?* which was very successful.

Woody Allen's career in movies was off and running. Two of his films, *Take the Money and Run* (1969) and *Bananas* (1971), became cult hits because of their dry, intellectual humor. One of his plays, *Play It Again, Sam*, was made into a movie in 1972.

Allen gained a reputation as an important filmmaker in 1975 with *Love and Death.* This film combines Allen's comic talent with his interest in philosophy and religion and his admiration for great filmmakers like Ingmar Bergman. Allen feels that *Love and Death* is his best film.

If *Love and Death* won Woody Allen respect, *Annie Hall* made him famous. But Allen did not stop there. Movies like *Stardust Memories* (1980), *Broadway Danny Rose* (1984), and *Hannah and Her Sisters* (1985) were bold attempts to blur the line between comedy and drama.

Woody Allen doesn't just make comedies; he makes classic movies that happen to be comedies. Allen is a brilliant filmmaker in any genre, and his place in movie history reaches far beyond his sense of humor.

Opposite: In *Play It Again, Sam,* **Allen pays tribute to movie legend Humphrey Bogart.**

For Further Reading

Bridges, Herb, and Terryl C. Boodman. *Gone with the Wind: The Definitive, Illustrated History of the Book, the Movie, the Legend.* New York: Fireside, 1989.

Meyer, Nicholas E. *Magic in the Dark: A Young Viewer's History of the Movies.* New York: Facts on File Publications, 1985.

Rothman, William. *Hitchcock: The Murderous Gaze.* Cambridge: Harvard University Press, 1982.

Sennett, Ted. *Great Hollywood Movies.* New York: Abradale Press, 1986.

Sinyard, Neil. *Classic Movies.* Manchester, New Hampshire: Salem House Publishers, 1985.

Spignesi, Stephen J. *The Woody Allen Companion.* Kansas City, Missouri: Andrews and McMeel, 1993.

Welles, Orson, and Peter Bogdanovich. *This Is Orson Welles.* New York: HarperCollins, 1993.

Index

Abel, Alfred, 11
Alland, William, 29
Allen, Woody, 10, 69, 70, 73, 77
Annie Hall, 69-77
Axelrod, George, 39, 41, 46, 47

Ball, Lucille, 26
Balsam, Martin, 49
Bananas, 77
Bergman, Ingmar, 77
Birth of a Nation, 9
Blade Runner, 18
Bloch, Robert, 49
Bonnie and Clyde, 66-67

Brando, Marlon, 59, 60, 61
Brickman, Marshall, 69, 70
Broadway Danny Rose, 77
Brooks, Albert, 70
Brown, Kay, 25

Caan, James, 59, 60
Cagney, James, 66
Cazale, John, 59
Chaplin, Charlie, 71, 72, 73
Citizen Kane, 9, 10, 29-37
Close Encounters of the Third Kind, 8-9
comedies, 70-73

Comingore, Dorothy, 29
Condon, Richard, 40, 41
Coppola, Francis Ford, 59, 60, 61, 62
Cotten, Joseph, 29
Curtis, Tony, 72

Dark Journey, 26
Davis, Bette, 26
Day, Doris, 72
Defending Your Life, 70
de Havilland, Olivia, 19
De Niro, Robert, 59, 60, 61
Douglas, Kirk, 40

Dracula, 57
Dr. Strangelove, or How I Learned to Stop Worrying and Love the Bomb, 73
Duck Soup, 72
Duvall, Robert, 59, 60

A Farewell to Arms, 28
Ford, Harrison, 18
Frankenheimer, John, 39, 40, 41, 46
Frankenstein, 57
Frohlich, Gustav, 11

Gable, Clark, 19
gangster movies, 66-67
Gavin, John, 49
The General, 71
George, Heinrich, 11
Godard, Jean-Luc, 9
The Godfather Epic, 59-67
Gone with the Wind, 10, 19-28
Gregory, James, 39
Griffith, D. W., 71

Hannah and Her Sisters, 77
Harvey, Laurence, 39, 40
Hearst, William Randolph, 31, 37
Heart of Darkness, 35
Helm, Brigitte, 11
Hepburn, Katharine, 26
Herrmann, Bernard, 50
Hitchcock, Alfred, 49-50
horror movies, 49, 57
Horse Feathers, 72
Howard, Leslie, 19

James Bond movies, 39

Karloff, Boris, 57
Keaton, Buster, 71, 73
Keaton, Diane, 59, 60, 69, 70
Kennedy, John F., 46
Keystone comedies, 71
Klein-Rogge, Rudolf, 11
Kubrick, Stanley, 73

Lancaster, Burt, 40

Lang, Fritz, 11, 13, 18
Lansbury, Angela, 39, 40
Leigh, Janet, 49, 50
Leigh, Vivien, 19, 26
Lewis, Jerry, 9, 72
Little Caesar, 66
Loos, Theodor, 11
Love and Death, 77

McCarthy, Joseph, 46
McGiver, John, 39
The Magnificent Ambersons, 37
The Manchurian Candidate, 39-47
Mankiewicz, Herman J., 29, 31, 36, 37
Martin, Dean, 72
Marx brothers, 72
*M*A*S*H,* 73
Menzies, William, 27, 28
Mercury Theater, 29, 35
Metropolis, 11-18
MGM Studios, 25, 27
Miles, Vera, 49
Mitchell, Margaret, 19, 25, 26

1984, 18

Orwell, George, 18

Pacino, Al, 59, 60-61
Paramount Pictures, 60
Parrish, Leslie, 39
Perkins, Anthony, 49, 50, 57
Play It Again, Sam, 77
Psycho, 49-57
The Public Enemy, 66
Puzo, Mario, 59

Rear Window, 49
Rebecca, 49
Redford, Robert, 40
Reiner, Rob, 70
RKO Studios, 29, 35
Roberts, Tony, 69
Robinson, Edward G., 66
Russo, Gianni, 59

science fiction movies, 9, 13, 18
Scorsese, Martin, 10
Selznick, David O., 19, 25, 26, 28
Seven Days in May, 40
Shadow of a Doubt, 49
Shelley, Mary, 57
Shire, Talia, 59
silent movies, 11, 71
Silva, Henry, 39
Sinatra, Frank, 39, 40, 46, 47
Sloan, Everett, 29
special effects, 13
spy movies, 39-40
Stardust Memories, 77
Stevenson, Robert Louis, 57
Stoker, Bram, 57
The Strange Case of Dr. Jekyll and Mr. Hyde, 57

Take the Money and Run, 77
Three Days of the Condor, 40
Touch of Evil, 37
The Tramp, 72

The War of the Worlds, 29, 35
Welles, Orson, 10, 29, 31-32, 35-37
Wells, H. G., 29
Wenders, Wim, 9
What's New, Pussycat?, 77
Wheeler, Lyle, 27
When Harry Met Sally, 70

Acknowledgments

Photographs reproduced with permission of Independent Picture Service, p. 1; Hollywood Book and Poster, pp. 2, 8, 15, 20, 23, 30, 36, 38, 43, 48, 51, 55, 56, 58, 63 (top and bottom), 67, 68, 70, 72; Wisconsin Center for Film and Theater Research, pp. 6, 16 (bottom), 44, 75, 80; Museum of Modern Art/Film Stills Archives, pp. 12, 16 (top), 24, 27, 33, 47, 52, 61; Cleveland Public Library, p. 76. Front cover: Hollywood Book and Poster. Back cover: Wisconsin Center for Film and Theater Research.